I Don't Want to go to Bed!

by
Julie Sykes

Illustrated by
Tim Warnes

tiger tales

Little Tiger did not like going to bed.
Every night when Mommy Tiger said,
"Bedtime!" Little Tiger would say,

"But I don't want
to go to bed!"

One night when Little Tiger said, "I don't want to go to bed!" Mommy roared, "All right! You can stay up all night long!" So Little Tiger scampered off into the jungle.

Little Tiger went to
visit his best friend,
who was having his
ears washed.

"Why are you still up?" growled
Daddy Lion.
"I don't want to go to bed!"
said Little Tiger. And he ran off
before Daddy Lion could wash
his ears, too!

Little Tiger went to visit
Little Elephant.

"Why are you still up?" trumpeted
Mommy Elephant.

"I don't want to go to bed!"
said Little Tiger, and he b o u n c e d
off before Mommy Elephant could
put him to bed, too!

Little Monkey was already
fast asleep.
"Why are you still up?"
whispered Mommy Monkey.

"I dont want to go to bed!" Little Tiger whispered back. And he tiptoed off before Mommy Monkey made him fall asleep, too!

Suddenly, it seemed very dark.
Little Tiger didn't know where to
go next. It was the first time
he had been in the jungle so late.

Little Tiger looked
up and saw. . .

...two very large yellow eyes staring back at him!

It was Bush Baby.
"Shouldn't you be in bed?"
she asked.
"I don't want to
go to bed,"
said Little Tiger,
shivering.

"Let's take you home," said Bush Baby.
"Your mommy will be worried about you."
"I don't want to go home!"
said Little Tiger.
But he didn't want to be left alone
in the dark, either.

So he followed Bush Baby through the jungle.

"Ah, there you are!" said Mommy Tiger.

"I don't want to go to..." yawned Little Tiger, and he fell fast asleep! Mommy Tiger tucked him in and turned to Bush Baby...

...but Bush Baby had disappeared into the jungle before Mommy Tiger could tuck her in, too!